The author, the illustrator
and the publisher
dedicate this book to:

Davy

Andreas François

Elia

Johannes.P Matteo

Gioia

Benoît

Anne Christian

Miša

... and all the children who ever want

and to all the Mamas who love them.

Kristina

Maleša

Samuel

Flo

Damjan

Johannes

atthias

Seli

Sascha

Bodula

Vàli

David

Jöni

Ulrich

now who Mama's favorite is

a minedition book
published by Penguin Young Readers Group

Original title: Mamas Liebling
English text translation by Kathryn Bishop
Coproduction with Michael Neugebauer Publishing Ltd., Hong Kong.
Rights arranged with "minedition"
Rights and Licensing AG, Zurich, Switzerland.

Published simultaneously in Canada.
Manufactured in Hong Kong by Wide World Ltd.
Typesetting in Goudy Old Style.
Color separation by Fotoreproduzioni Grafiche, Verona, Italy.

Library of Congress Cataloging-in-Publication Data available upon request.

ISBN 978-0-698-40076-4
10 9 8 7 6 5 4 3 2 1
First Impression

For more information please visit our website: www.minedition.com

Mama's Favorite

Brigitte Sidjanski  Sarah Emmanuelle Burg

minedition

Muri, a little mouse,
had a very loving mother.

He also had brothers and sisters.
Many brothers and sisters.
And he also had...

... a Papa.

Muri was never alone.

Sometimes he wondered, "Who is Mama's favorite?"

Mama's favorite must be his baby sister.
She always got an extra piece of cheese.
"She still has a lot of growing to do," explained Mama.

Muri tried to act as small and helpless as his baby sister.
But that didn't make Mama happy.
She only said, "Now Muri,
stop that nonsense, please!"

Muri's oldest sister lived far away.
Mama often sent her cheese and nuts.

When Mama got a letter from her, she read it a thousand times,
until it was covered with smudges and greasy fingerprints.
She didn't seem to have time for anyone else then.

Bhüet Di !
♡lich

So Muri decided he should go far away, too.
He put on his boots and started to go.
He closed the door loudly behind him.
He did it once and then tried it a second time.
"Mama, I'm leaving!" he shouted.
Mama just sighed and said,
"Sweetheart, please stop all that running back and forth."

One day Muri's older brother was sick.
Mama took care of him and stayed with him the whole time.
"Ah ha," thought Muri, "that's how you get to be Mama's favorite."
"Mama," he said. "I have an awful stomachache."
"Well, when you have a stomachache,
you shouldn't have anything else to eat,"
said Mama.

MINEDITION

Oh my, only herbal tea for Muri.
Poor, poor Muri!

A few days later his little sister came running to Mama crying. She had lost her favorite kerchief.

"I'll help you look for it, sweetheart, don't worry," said Mama. "And until we find it, put this daisy behind your ear. It looks pretty."

SOAP

Suddenly Muri cried,
"Mama, I've lost my scarf!"
Mama looked over at him and smiled mischievously.
"So, you've lost your scarf," Mama said. "Well, you'd better go look for it. I'm sure you'll find it, sweetheart."

That same evening Mama called Muri:

"I'm going to take a walk, would you like to come along?"

Muri beamed.

They had just started when they saw ...

... a cat!

Like lightning Mama grabbed Muri and ran away.

They were safe.

Mama put Muri in her lap and hugged him.
She whispered softly in his ear,
"It's all right sweetheart, everything is all right."

Then everything really was all right,
for everyone. Mama was the best,
and Muri understood that she
loved them all the same.